You Can Be Kind, Pout-Pout Fish!

Deborah Diesen

Pictures by Greg Paprocki, based on illustrations
created by Dan Hanna for the *New York Times*–
bestselling Pout-Pout Fish books

Farrar Straus Giroux
New York

Farrar Straus Giroux Books for Young Readers
An imprint of Macmillan Publishing Group, LLC
120 Broadway, New York, NY 10271

Text copyright © 2020 by Deborah Diesen
Pictures copyright © 2020 by Farrar Straus Giroux Books for Young Readers
All rights reserved
Color separations by Embassy Graphics
Printed in China by RR Donnelley Asia Printing Solutions Ltd.,
Dongguan City, Guangdong Province
Designed by Aram Kim
First edition, 2020

3 5 7 9 10 8 6 4 2

mackids.com

Library of Congress Control Number: 2019940839

Hardcover ISBN: 978-0-374-31292-3
Paperback ISBN: 978-0-374-31293-0

Our books may be purchased in bulk for promotional, educational, or business use.
Please contact your local bookseller or the Macmillan Corporate and Premium Sales Department
at (800) 221-7945 ext. 5442 or by email at MacmillanSpecialMarkets@macmillan.com.

Mr. Fish was about to pout.

One friend was unhappy.
Then two friends were.

Then three.
Then four!

Soon, the whole class was
in a bad mood.
The bad mood was big.
No one had a smile.
No one had a laugh.

Mr. Fish sank down.

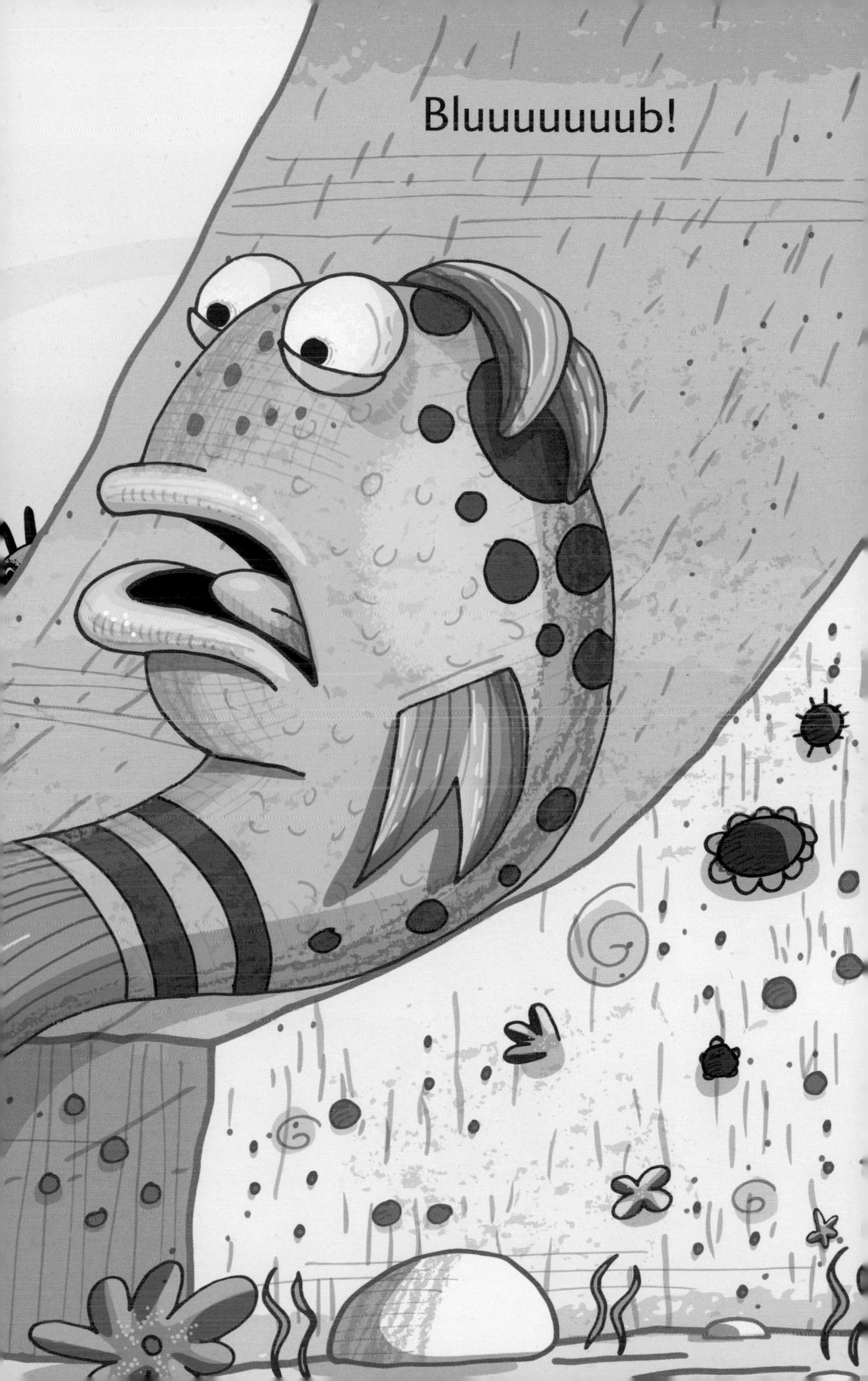
Bluuuuuuub!

"I do not know what to do."

He looked around.

"One fish cannot change this."

Then he had an idea.

He tried it.

It worked!

He tried it again, in a new way.

It worked!

He tried it again, in a new way.

It worked again!

He kept trying.

Every time he tried, it worked.

It was not hard.

It was not hard to *be kind*.

His idea spread.

One friend was kind.

Then two friends were. Then three.

Then four!

Soon, the whole class was in
a good mood.

"I can be kind!" said Mr. Fish.

"We *all* can be kind," said the class.

"No pout about it!"